C000202980

When not writing, John Offord is a political campaigner. Firstly, to adopt the tried and successful jury system for selection of the cabinet, so 12 citizens chosen at random would replace the present cabinet, currently chosen by a tried and unsuccessful system.

Secondly, to get Robert Louis Stevenson recognised as the founder of the EU. RLS is remembered for famously crossing Europe with a donkey.

John's proudest achievement was winning a prize in the prestigious Sunday Times Chess Competition. The problem posed was: "White appears to be in a commanding position but black has a surprising killer move. Can you see it?" John gave the correct answer which was "No" and after some correspondence he was given the prize.

To Jo – with thanks for the butterflies.

John Offord

Bees Make Honey and Butterflies Make Jam

AUSTIN MACAULEY PUBLISHERS™
LONDON • CAMBRIDGE • NEW YORK • SHARJAH

This is a work of fiction. Names, characters, businesses, places, events, locales, and incidents are either the products of the author's imagination or used in a fictitious manner. Any resemblance to actual persons, living or dead, or actual events is purely coincidental.

A CIP catalogue record for this title is available from the British Library.

ISBN 9781398416307 (Paperback)
ISBN 9781398416314 (Hardback)
ISBN 9781398416321 (ePub e-book)

www.austinmacauley.com

First Published 2022
Austin Macauley Publishers Ltd®
1 Canada Square
Canary Wharf
London
E14 5AA

Acknowledgements

My thanks to many kings and queens for a plenteous supply of princesses, without whom this book could not have been written.

My thanks to the Women's Institute for the valuable insight into their activities, notably nude calendars and the boiling of Brussels sprouts. This book may be seen by children so there are no illustrations of Brussels sprouts.

My thanks to my daughter, Joanne, for the title of this book.

She was three years old when I told her where honey comes from, and not to be outdone in making up improbable stories, she replied, "And butterflies make jam." So, I borrowed that for the title of this book. Thank you, Jo.

My thanks to Matt Boulton, one-time classmate of my daughter Hazel, for the cover illustration. He refused payment maintaining it was recompense for the damage done to our house by their teenage parties.

Table of Contents

No princesses were harmed in the production of this book,
except on page 13

The Beautiful Princess

Once upon a time, there was a beautiful princess. She was not only a beautiful princess, she was a dutiful beautiful princess. She ran a charity for stray animals, she was captain of her school football team, her bedroom was tidy, and she always did her homework on time. Her hair was brushed, her fingernails were clean, and she was never cheeky to her parents.

One day when she was walking in the woods she fell in the lake and drowned.

Health and Hygiene

It frightened me when my brother came home from biology class and told me there were more germs on our dishcloth than there were on our toilet seat. I thought of my poor mother handling this dishcloth and I thought of the dishes being washed with it and then we ate off them. It frightened me and I could not sleep. But not anymore because now I know it is not true.

I know it is not true because now if I can't sleep, I creep out and wipe the toilet seat with the dishcloth.

Buttons and Buttonholes

"You can't go to school like that," said Mother. "Your blouse is all lopsided where you haven't done the buttons up evenly."

"It's not my fault," said Priscilla. "One of the buttonholes fell out and rolled under the bed so I had more buttons than buttonholes and it went all crooked."

"Your father has a hole in his sock that I am sure he could spare," said Mother. "We will take that and put it in your blouse then you can look neat again."

"Hurrah!" said Priscilla. But, oh dear, the blouse was pink and the socks were blue so the hole was the wrong colour and they had to put it back in the sock.

"If you cut off one button," said Mother, "the buttons and buttonholes will match."

As Priscilla did this the button fell down and also rolled under the bed but no one cared because the buttons and buttonholes now matched and Priscilla could go neatly to school.

In the darkness under the bed, the button slid quietly into the buttonhole.

The Little Mouse

Once upon a time, there was a little mouse. He was very poor, poor as a church mouse. Too poor to buy the ice-cream that was his favourite food. One day he had an idea and said to his friends, "I will rob a bank, then I will have enough money to buy ice-cream."

"Hurrah!" said all his friends.

"You will have to wear a suit if you are going to the bank," said Mrs Mouse. So he put on his best suit and a smart tie, but, oh dear, when he came back, he was looking very unhappy.

"Did you get lots of money?" asked all his friends.

"No," said the little mouse. "The queue was so big, I gave up and came away with nothing, zilch, zero."

"Oh!" said all his friends.

"I have an idea," said Mrs Mouse, "if we take the zero that you came away with, we can stick it on the end of our bank statement and then we will have ten times as much money and can buy lots of ice-cream."

"Hurrah!" cried all their friends.

But, oh dear, they had forgotten that they had an overdraft so they had made their overdraft ten times as big.

"You must come and see me," said the bank manager, "to explain why your overdraft is so big."

"I have an idea," said Mrs Mouse. "I will go and complain that our overdraft has suddenly grown although we have not bought any ice-cream."

"You will need to take your big handbag and your big umbrella," said Little Mouse.

So Mrs Mouse took her big handbag and her big umbrella and complained. "There is a bank error in your favour," she said.

"They always are," said the bank manager but then he saw her big handbag and her big umbrella and said, "Sorry, Mrs Mouse, I will make sure it never happens again."

So he filled in a big form to stop it happening again, but he kept glancing at the big handbag and the big umbrella instead of the big form so he got it wrong and stopped their account from ever showing an overdraft. So however much ice-cream they bought they always stayed in credit.

So Little Mouse and Mrs Mouse and their friends bought lots and lots of ice-cream and got very fat and they died of being fat.

Saint Peter decided that because they had put one over on the bank they should go straight to heaven. In Mouse Heaven they have cats as servants so every day the mice sent the cats out for ice-cream and lived happily ever after.

The Stolen Wellington Boots

Once upon a time, there was a beautiful princess. All was well in the Kingdom except the king was unhappy because his Wellington boots kept getting stolen. He would step out of the door thinking he was stepping into his Wellington boots but instead would step into a muddy puddle and be very cross. So he issued a proclamation that anyone who could solve the mystery of the stolen Wellington boots would receive his daughter's hand in marriage.

Many princes tried, but always if they looked away for a moment the boots would be gone and the king would again step into the muddy puddle and be cross. A famous Professor of Wellington Boots researched the problem and advised the king, "Instead of leaving your boots tidy, with the left one on the left and the right one on the right, put them the other way round then anyone who steals them will find them so uncomfortable they will immediately bring them back."

So the king followed this advice and next day was delighted to find his boots in place where he had left them.

"Hurrah!" said the famous Professor of Wellington Boots. "Now I will marry the beautiful princess."

"Read the small print," said the king. "It is my ugly daughter, Princess Stroppy, whose hand I offered in marriage."

So the famous Professor of Wellington Boots married the ugly princess and he was always cross that he had been caught out by the small print, and she was always cross because he kept calling her Princess Ugly. So they argued a lot but luckily they both liked arguing and so they lived happily ever after.

To Space and Back

“What did those pink-faced desk drivers back at base know about driving a spaceship?” mused red-haired Hank McLuke, a wide grin spreading across his freckled face as he eased the throttle up another notch.

“Don’t exceed warp five in a 20-year-old spaceship,” was their latest instruction as though they knew better how to handle a spaceship than a man who had been ferrying between the galaxies for 25 years.

He eased up to warp six and the spaceship disintegrated and became another bit of space junk along with the more resilient parts of Hank McLuke’s spacesuit.

The Lights

In the middle of Cornwall was a little village whose name no one could remember. They had no streetlights so the nights were dark and showed up the coloured lights droning across the sky. The people were afraid of the lights. Some said they were witches riding their broomsticks. Some said they were the eyes of giant owls that would swoop down and carry people away. So the people were too afraid to go out at night. The husbands were unhappy because they could not go to the pub but had to stay in and do Conversation. The wives were unhappy because they could not go to the Women's Institute to discuss the boiling of Brussels sprouts while posing nude for calendars.

Meanwhile, 4,000 miles away an important event was taking place. Mrs Wright said to Mr Wright, "You put the baby to bed and I'll get out the oysters and champagne."

Twenty-four years of restraint passed in the little village whose name no one could remember. Suddenly the Wright brothers discovered The Aeroplane! Then everyone knew that the droning lights were harmless aeroplanes crossing the night sky and so it was safe to go out at night. The husbands went to the pub every night and the wives went to the Women's Institute to discuss the boiling of Brussels sprouts while posing nude for calendars. But still all was not well. Some of the husbands complained about soggy Brussels sprouts (but not about the nude calendars). And some of the wives complained that the husbands spent too much time at the pub. This called for a bit of wife swapping and then they all lived happily ever after.

I Think They Liked Me

I've always wanted to work in one of them big office's with big glass doors and everything and I think I've got the job! They were very friendly at the interview and smiled a lot. They asked for my Sea View so I explained that I lived in Dalston Junction with no sea and they seemed very happy with that, smiled a lot.

They asked me about filing so I explained that I start with the thumb on my left hand and work round very systematically all the other fingers then go on to the right hand which of course is a bit more difficult. They smiled a lot again and asked about the other kind of filing and I enlightened them with my system for that as well. I said I thought filing was very important (I'm a great diplomat!!!) so I never did it on a Monday when I might be tired or on a Friday when I mostly phoned my boyfriend so I usually do it on a Tuesday.

I have three drawers, neatly labelled Miscellaneous, General and Not Sure. Being a careful person, I like to have a Not Sure drawer because it would not do to put something in Miscellaneous when it belonged in General. They smiled a lot again, I think they liked me. But just then I wasn't sure if I wanted to work for them because they choked a lot and one of them kept going out of the room, but Mum said that would be the air conditioning so that's alright, but I'd already decided that three lifts that went very fast made up for the choking.

Anyway, I explained that I meticulously file things by date according to the day I do the filing. So there are three divisions in each drawer, neatly labelled Tuesday, Wednesday and Thursday. Tuesday is the fattest because that's the day I mostly do the filing. They smiled a lot again and the young one seemed to want me to go on explaining things to them, but I said I would give them my expertise when I worked for them.

I think they liked me.

The Mitsikini Invasion

Princess Hannah was just drifting off to a dreamy sleep when she thought she heard a tapping at her window. *Tap tapetty tap-tap – tap-tap* it went.

"I know that tap," thought Princess Hannah, *"it's my friend Yanyi from Mars."* So she opened her window and there was Yanyi with his little spaceship and looking worried.

"Can you help?" said Yanyi. "We are being invaded by the Mitsikini people who are made entirely of bottoms and elbows, and they barge with their bottoms and prod with their elbows making life very uncomfortable for us peace-loving Martians."

"Of course," said Hannah. "First take me in your spaceship to my friend Sheila in Australia."

"Hello, Sheila," said Hannah when they landed. "Can you help us?"

"Fair dinkum," said Sheila.

"Can we please have a bit of your back garden?"

"Fair dinkum," said Sheila and helped load a chunk of her garden into Yanyi's spaceship.

"Thanks," said Yanyi.

"Fair dinkum," said Sheila.

Back on Mars, locating the Mitsikini spaceship was difficult because Martian miles go round in circles instead of straight lines and Martian kilometres are just as bad with a break in the middle so that when you get halfway along you have to search around for the second half. But they found the Mitsikinis just in time to see them barging their way past the Martians and climbing into their spaceship for the night.

"Put Sheila's garden under their spaceship," said Hannah. "It has the negative gravity that prevents Australians from falling off the bottom of the Earth."

No sooner had they done that than the negative gravity sent the Mitsikini spaceship zooming off into space, never to be seen again.

"We must get you back in time for school," said Yanyi. "Just time to fly round to the back of Mars and the Mars Bar mines for your refreshment on the journey home."

"Time to get up, sleepy head," said Mother. "Or you'll be late for school."

"Oh Mum, I'm so sleepy, I've been across the Solar System all night," muttered Hannah.

"No, you've been dreaming about Yanyi again," said Mother. "Just get ready for school – but first pick up those Mars Bar wrappers. Where on Earth did they come from?"

"Where on Earth?" said Hannah.

The Princess and the Frog

Once upon a time, there was a beautiful princess called Princess Hannah and one day when she was walking through the woods, she saw in a clearing a frog sitting on a toadstool and wearing a crown.

"*Bonjour!*" said the frog. "*Comment t'appelle tu?*"

"My name is Hannah," said the princess.

"Ah, Anna, *tres joli,*" said the frog.

"Not Anna, Hannah," said Hannah.

"*Oui, comme j'ai dit,* Anna," said the frog.

Princess Hannah was getting tired of this conversation so she said,

"Why are you wearing a crown?"

"*Parce que vraiment je ne suis pas un frog. Je suis un andsome prince, le Prince de Thailand et de Siam, et quand une princesse moi marrie je serais encore un andsome prince,*" replied the frog.

"Thailand and Siam are the same place, just two different names, you just try to make it sound grander," said the princess.

The frog was getting tired of this conversation so he said,

"If you will marry me, I will take you to my Kingdom of Siam."

“Oogle boogle goo,” said the princess who had just remembered she was only six months old and that was all she could say. The frog was not much good at English either and he took this as agreement to marry him. So on her eighteenth birthday they were married and the frog immediately turned into un andsome prince and they went to Siam where he eventually became king.

So Hannah and the King of Siam lived happily ever after, supplementing their Royal salary by singing songs from their show.

Soul Mates

It took thousands of generations for evolution to transform amoebae to the first mammals and thousands more to produce a humanoid. We do not know what it took for the first of these to acquire a soul. As befits the first man to have a soul he lived a blameless life and this ensured his soul went straight to Heaven – the first to do so. As he walked through Heaven's gate he was greeted with a smile and outstretched hands.

"Welcome to Heaven," said Adam. "We've been waiting for you."

How the Land Was Formed on Planet Earth

In her day, many years ago, Princess Cresty, the giant-crested whale, was the biggest creature in all the lakes and seas and oceans. Which meant she was the biggest creature on the planet, because at that time it was nearly all sea with not much land and therefore not many land creatures.

Although it was the biggest creature that ever lived, not much is known about the giant-crested whale, partly because it was too big to see with the naked eye, partly because immediately after mating their mate ate them. Not like some spiders where the lady spider eats the gentleman spider – giant-crested whales formed a circle, head to tail, and went *chomp, chomp, chomp* until there was nothing left.

The little we know of them comes from their migrating habits. When they got fed up living at home, they migrated across to the far side of the ocean and kept in touch with great booming notes that echoed across the ocean. Now although there were not many land creatures at that time, there were some at Bletchley Park and they got hold of one of Princess Cresty's great booming notes and deciphered it and it said, "My flatmate is a pig. She does no washing up and she eats all my cornflakes. If I come home, can I bring my laundry?"

When she sent that note, she did not wait for an answer but sped across the ocean at top speed. In going so fast she let out a great burp that floated up to the atmosphere where the methane caused global warming that evaporated one third of the oceans, exposing the land where we live today.

Thank you, Princess Cresty.

Advertisement

For Sale!

Magic Carpet You just drop your clothes on it and next day they reappear clean and ready to wear in your wardrobe or chest of drawers.

And

Magic Table
Even faster. You just sit down at it, open your newspaper and food appears by magic.

Both still working perfectly after 25 years. I am reluctant to sell but I have a special friend with expensive tastes.
Available from The Royalties Payments Manager, Austin Macauley Pubishers.

Advertisement

We've all had the experience – you pack a picnic, the hamper is full and you realise you need to take another sandwich. Now there is a solution!!!

The Iron-on Sandwich!!!

Simply iron on to any convenient part of your person and when it is needed, quickly remove with the handy Iron-on Sandwich Removal Tool.
Enjoy today's special offer, two for the price of three, and be the envy of all your friends.

Advertisement

The world's best book: *Bees Make Honey and Butterflies Make Jam*
The Perfect Christmas gift for all your friends

- Cheap
- Looks Expensive
- Fits in a C4 envelope. As easy to pack as a Christmas Card.
- The cover is varnished so your less literate friends can use it as a coaster.
- Available from all good booksellers.

Optional: Remove this page before posting.

Index